Kids Tag

Just Right Reader

Big kids like to tag.

Tim tags Dan.

Dan zigs to tag Kim.

Kim tags Ann.

Jim zigs.

Jim zags.

Ann zips to tag him.

Can Jim tag Kim?

No.

Jim taps Tim.

Big kids like to tag.

Phonics Fun

- Use magnetic letters or create your own on individual squares of paper: b, d, i, g, h, k, m, z.
- Use the letters to make words from the list.
- Make and read each word.

big   him   kid   zig

Comprehension

How did Tim behave at the beginning of the story?

Decodable Words

big	Kim
him	Tim
Jim	zig
kid	zip

15